NOBLE-HEARTED KATE

NOBLE-HEARTED KATE

A Celtic Tale

by

MARIANNA MAYER

with illustrations by
WINSLOW PELS

A BANTAM SKYLARK BOOK®
NEW YORK · TORONTO · LONDON · SYDNEY · AUCKLAND

I would like to thank a most generous librarian, Margaret Sax, at the Watkinson Library, Trinity College, for her kindness in supplying me with early background material for this project.

For Poo, prince of swans   —W.P.

NOBLE-HEARTED KATE

A Bantam Skylark Book / November 1990

Skylark Books is a registered trademark of Bantam Books, a division of Bantam Doubleday Dell Publishing Group, Inc. Registered in U.S. Patent and Trademark Office and elsewhere.

Library of Congress Cataloging-in-Publication Data

Mayer, Marianna.
    Noble-hearted Kate : a Celtic tale / by Marianna Mayer ; with illustrations by Winslow Pels.
        p.   cm.
    "A Bantam Skylark book."
    Summary: Using elements of traditional Celtic lore, relates how Kate helps her stepsister Meghan to break the spell that has given her the head of a sheep.
    ISBN 0-553-07049-5
    [1. Fairy tales.]   I. Pels, Winslow   ill.
    II. Title.
    PZ8.M4514No   1990
    [Fic]—dc20   90-640
                                                                  CIP
                                                                  AC

Published simultaneously in the United States and Canada

PRINTED IN THE UNITED STATES OF AMERICA

RAD   0 9 8 7 6 5 4 3 2 1

Preface

ONCE UPON A TIME, fairy tales, folk-tales, and myths were for everyone. It is a relatively recent assumption that they are reserved for children exclusively. Indeed, from time immemorial the storyteller gathered listeners around the open hearth to tell tales rich in culture and tradition. They took the old stories, the myths, legends, and lore, and wove them with a freshness and clarity that spoke to their audience. In this way no story ever remained the same for very long, but changed and developed instead to suit the time and the teller's imagination.

Noble-Hearted Kate comes from such a tradition of storytelling. As *Kate Crackernut* it was an Orcadian oral tale (from the Orkney Islands of Scotland), collected by D. J. Robertson and published in *Folk-Lore* (Vol. 1, September 1890). In its first form it is the unusual tale of enchantment and disenchantment and the power of Faeries to draw mortals into their hills and to wear out their lives with dancing. Nine years ago I found the tale in a book that included numerous folklore motifs, but only a be-

ginning and an end were given, with nothing in between. At that time I was researching another story, but I filed away the idea this fragment inspired in me.

Who was this girl Kate, I wondered, who could save a young man from the Faeries and who could love a stepsister more beautiful than she? How did all this work within the context of the stereotypes of the wicked stepsister and the young hero who saves the maiden in distress?

I longed to know how the story would come out, and so years later I sat down to write my own story of Kate and Meghan in order to find out. Once begun, the story produced an array of intriguing elements from Celtic lore that emerged as my cast of characters: the age-old, one-eyed Salmon of Wisdom, who appears and disappears in countless Celtic legends; the salamander, a Faerie sprite believed to make his sultry home within the burning flames; and the tree the Celts called the Tree of Knowledge, the hazelnut. The *Old Irish Tree Alphabet* names the hazelnut tree the ninth sacred tree and the symbol of the ninth month.

The wealth of folklore surrounding the *sidhe*, pronounced "shee," also became a powerful influence throughout the story. The *sidhe* is the group of pagan gods and goddesses belonging to the ancient Celts. Today they have been reduced to playful sprites or Faeries who perform benign magic in chil-

dren's stories. But when the *sidhe* first walked the land that is now England, Scotland, Ireland, and Wales, they were awesome creatures terrible in their beauty and power. In time they were to disappear, making their home underground or within woodland hills and mounds.

Nevertheless, the list of their remaining influence is long. The Faerie mist (*ceo sidhe*) wherein a mortal can go astray. Faerie music (*ceol sidhe*) sometimes heard as the tinkling of bells lures mortals into the Faerie world. Faerie sleep (*suan sidhe*) is a sleep from which one cannot wake. The faerie host (*sluag sidhe*), which represents the company of riders riding upon a Faerie wind (*seidean sidhe*), which can carry magic hither and yon. Magic was everywhere, or so the Celts believed. It roamed free through the natural wood, and mysterious powers were always at play.

Lastly the beautiful Scottish ballad "Tam Lin" played a part, for it follows a number of familiar folklore motifs belonging to Kate.

Finally I set the task to create a fresh tale, motivated by these elements but not rigidly based on material of the past. Instead, all the stories in the Timeless Tales series are original, using old tradition as their source of inspiration. For this reason *Noble-Hearted Kate* and the other tales in the series should be read not as works of scholarship or adaptation but as works of pure imagination.

MARIANNA MAYER

Chapter One

NCE THERE WAS a king who lived in the east and a queen who lived in the west. They each had a wish to marry and they each had a daughter born the same day, hour, and year! Letters flew back and forth from the kingdom in the east to the kingdom in the west and vice versa. Soon the king and queen were wed, and they took up residence in the king's splendid castle.

Years passed and the stepsisters grew tall and bright and pretty. Their tie of love was stronger than that of blood, and if one was looked for, then the other was sure to be found, for they were seldom separated. The king's daughter, Meghan, had eyes the color of blue cornflowers and hair as yellow as golden wheat. The queen's own daughter, Kate, had long flame-red hair and eyes so green a cat might envy her. Truly they were as alike as sunlight and sunset in beauty and in spirit. But for all that, it seemed to the queen that the king's daughter was far more beautiful than her own sweet Kate. Indeed, the otherwise quite reasonable gentlewoman

pondered this fact for some time, and the more she thought of it the worse she felt about it.

At last, the matter so disturbed her peace of mind that she found her way to the secluded hut of an old woman whom some called a witch to ask advice.

"Tell me, old woman, how can I make my daughter more beautiful? Kate's too plain and her stepsister, Meghan, outshines her. I'm quite beside myself as to what to do about it," concluded the queen with a wild look in her eye. Indeed, at that moment she looked as though she might do anything at all that came into her head.

"Well, my dear. It's very difficult for a witch like myself to make things better, but I can certainly make things *worse*. Suppose'n Meghan should *fail* to shine, then your own sweet Kate will be very pretty by comparison," reasoned the old woman.

The queen was delighted, and in exchange for a small purse of gold coins she was given some herbs to place beneath Meghan's pillow while the girl slept.

That very night, when the candles were blown out and everyone in the castle was sound asleep, the queen crept from her bed and stepped noiselessly down the long, dark hall. In no time the queen slipped the herbs under Meghan's pillow and was back in her own chamber without anyone being the wiser.

Now, the old woman's magic might have failed but for the fact that tonight was a special night, the Eve of Samhain, known to us as All Hallows' Eve. At midnight on this night, the spirits of Faerie roam free and have ears to listen to the wishes of mortals and sometimes on a whim may grant or ignore them.

The next morning Meghan awoke shrieking in distress. Kate came running and burst into the room. What she saw broke Kate's heart, for poor Meghan had a sheep's head in place of her own.

The queen couldn't have been more pleased, though she concealed it from everyone. She wept as loud as the rest and wrung her hands in great despair. But Kate knew her mother too well to be deceived. She loved her stepsister with all her heart— there was not one jealous bone in her—and she was determined that somehow she would set things right.

When she was sure they were quite alone, Kate wrapped Meghan's head with a soft linen scarf, and as she did she spoke soothingly, saying, "In the days long gone by, before either of us was born, there once was a cool, dark river that ran the length of the land. At one end, near the very edge of the riverbank, a hazelnut tree grew. It was thought to be the true Tree of Knowledge, and people said that whoever ate these hazelnuts grew wise. A great fish, a salmon with one eye, lived in the river. Indeed, for all we know, my dear Meghan, he may live there still. I for one believe he does.

"He would be very ancient now, for even then he was older than the oldest being in the world and wiser than anyone, human or animal. He knew the names of the stars and their movements, the whole history of the world, and what's more he could foretell the future. The cause of his great wisdom was that year after year, since the beginning of the world, the nuts from the hazel tree fell one by one into the water, and each one that fell was eaten by the wise salmon.

"When I was a wee babe, my nurse often told me the tale before bedtime, for I loved to hear it. Now, Meghan, I think we must go in search of the Salmon of Wisdom. It is his wisdom that we need. If we can find him, I know he will tell me what must be done so that I can help you. It is our only hope. Say you will come with me, and together we will leave here and go out into the world."

Meghan pressed her stepsister's hand with her own and tried to smile. "Aye, my dear, sweet Kate. I will gladly go with you," she told her.

But it would be no easy task to find the Salmon of Wisdom, and in their hearts both girls knew this, although neither spoke of it to the other. They might well harbor doubts, for only the wise and the very good can find the salmon and talk with him. Indeed, many have gone in search of him, and though they might spend the whole of their lives looking, very few ever found him. And then those

who were successful did not always have enough faith within themselves to understand his words, for the Salmon of Wisdom never gives advice.

Nevertheless, their minds were made up, and the two sisters started on their journey early the next day on the most glorious of mornings, with the moon still aglow and the owls hooting in the wood. They went on foot, and as they walked the moon faded and the sun came up, but the moon rose again before they stopped to rest for the night.

Day after day, they traveled on and on, until one afternoon they came upon a river, and there at the water's edge a little green-and-blue boat was moored.

When the sisters saw the boat, they wanted nothing more than to take it down the river. Kate untied the rope and the two climbed aboard. No sooner were they seated than the boat began to drift, and carried by the current of the river, it floated slowly on. Although there were no oars or pole to guide them, somehow they were not afraid. Instead, their hearts were at ease. Soon they felt quite drowsy, and in a dreamlike calm they trailed their fingers in the cool, dark water. Each smiled at the other, and from time to time they breathed a soft sigh of contentment as they drifted.

But then, in a little while, a change came over Meghan. She grew restless and uneasy. Finally, she sat up and told Kate, "Something is very wrong

here. Don't ask me how I know, for I can't explain. But there is a great fish at the river bottom and he is in grave danger. The tall reeds that grow in the riverbed have got hold of him. And if we don't do something, he is sure to perish."

Kate looked down at the river. The water was so black that it was impossible to see down to the bottom. But she trusted Meghan, and she said, "Well, then, you must tell me where to find him, for the river is long and it is running quickly."

"Here, now," answered Meghan, pointing to a spot in the river. "The fish is trapped just there. Don't be afraid, but mind you take care. The reeds are thick and nasty. They have a mind of their own and it's none too nice, I'm afraid."

Kate jumped. The water was cold and very black, but soon she saw light shining through a mass of thick, dark-green reeds. Swaying this way and that, the reeds were like a thousand evil-looking tentacles ready to clasp her in their grip if she ventured too close. Never mind, she told herself, I will not show them that I'm afraid. Perhaps if I appear brave, they will not know how really frightened I am.

With this in mind she swam toward the light up ahead. Sure enough, just as Meghan had assured her, there among the reeds a fish lay trapped. The light that shone like a great beacon in the darkness was his alone.

16

When she reached him, Kate hurried to cut away the tangle of reeds. But they began to take hold of her. At first she tried to brush them away, but more drew around her. Like snakes they clutched at her legs, her hands, her hair, and her face. Tearing at them, she kept up her struggle to free the fish till she thought her heart would burst for want of air. Finally, thanks to her, he broke loose. Only then did Kate think of her own safety. Still holding her breath, she managed to wrench free. At last she swam away and made for the surface. With her lungs burning, she burst out of the water. Quickly Meghan reached down, took hold of Kate's hands, and pulled her into the boat.

The fish had also come to the surface. He was watching them from a distance, and as their boat drifted so did he, but always keeping far enough away to be out of sight. He did not draw closer for a long while, but when he saw that Kate had caught her breath and was quite settled, slowly he swam toward them.

"I shall never forget your kindness to me," said the fish when he was just beside the boat.

The girls turned and looked at him. He was a great fish, a salmon with one eye, and they had saved his life, or so it seemed.

Chapter Two

T WAS MY SISTER, Meghan, who saw that you were in trouble. But how she knew, neither of us can say," Kate told the salmon.

A quick glance passed between the stepsisters. They were both wondering the same thing. Was this fish the salmon they were seeking? If he was, both girls could not believe their good luck. But they dared not ask him outright; it would be impolite, and they wouldn't risk offending him for all the world. No, they were in silent agreement, they would not ask.

"I see," replied the fish. The girls waited, he seemed about to speak again. Even above water, Kate marveled at him. His scales shimmered, and she thought the light actually came from inside him. But how is that possible? she wondered.

Finally, he said, "Though you call Meghan your sister, aren't you both stepsisters?" When the girls nodded yes, he went on. "But you're like sisters, for you are truly devoted to each other. Yes, I see that clearly. It is a good thing among people to

19

care for each other. A very good thing indeed."
Then he was silent again.

He spoke so softly, it was as though he was
dreaming while he spoke, and the girls had to strain
if they were to hear him. Then when he did stop
speaking, his words trailed off like ripples upon the
water, making the girls think it was they themselves
who were dreaming. Kate wondered suddenly if she
was dreaming of him or if he was dreaming of her.
Surely it was as though they or he were not really
real.

To shake off this strange feeling, Kate broke
the silence, saying, "Oh, yes. We do love each
other."

"We could not be closer," said Meghan from
behind the linen scarf she still wore around her
head.

"And that's why we are seeking the Salmon of
Wisdom. You see, under this scarf, Meghan has the
head of a sheep. She hasn't always had it," said
Kate.

"No, I should say not!" added Meghan.

"But not too many days ago she woke up, and
there it was upon her shoulders instead of her own
beautiful head!" Kate continued. "So we decided to
leave home in search of him. We hope he can tell
us what we must do."

"Ahh," said the fish as he slowly bobbed up
and down in the water. "Yes, the Salmon of Wis-

dom, hmm. But he is very shy, you know. No one ever sees him anymore. The world's changed since he was in his prime. Now people don't go seeking for answers. They don't even seem to have questions anymore. Now the reeds at the bottom of the river rule the river just as reason rules the world. And it appears that even a great fish can fall victim to such power if he is not forever on his guard. Then, if he's to get free, he must rely on the kindness of two innocent girls. Oh, dear, yes. The world has changed while I've lived in this river. The reeds are a good example of that." His thoughts began to drift again, and the girls imagined he might be falling asleep.

But, no. All at once he caught himself, and he asked, "Tell me, though. Are there still stories about the salmon? I fancied he'd long been forgotten."

"Oh, yes!" they exclaimed, hoping to reassure him.

"Kate's nurse told her about him when she was very young, as did my own nurse while I was a child," Meghan explained.

"How nice," said the salmon, and they could see he meant it.

After a pause he began again, "I'm thinking, Meghan, that it's not such a bad thing to have the head of a sheep. Are you surprised that I should think so?" Clearly, both Meghan and Kate were surprised.

"Well, listen," continued the salmon. "I'm reminded of a lesson I learned once, long ago. It's just this, when you lose something precious you always gain something else. I don't mean that since you've lost your head, at least, you've gained another. No, no, not that. Instead, I'm suggesting that you've gained a whole new way of seeing. For example, I don't think you would have known about my troubles down among the reeds, if not for this extraordinary change in you."

Now it was Meghan's turn to be silent as she thought this over. Finally, she said, "I admit things do seem different to me. It's as if I have a kind of second sight now. As though I can see beyond what's on the surface. I'm glad for such a talent and I'm glad that we were able to save you because of it. But I don't want to have the head of a sheep the rest of my life. I am a girl, after all."

"Oh, dear, yes. Of course you are, my soul," said the salmon in the most kindly voice. "I am only suggesting, only venturing a theory, you see, for you to ponder when you wish to, that having experienced such a loss may provide its own advantage. That is, if you are willing to recognize it.

"And yet, you do wish your own head back. I do see your point, of course. Oh, my, yes, I do. Now, if I was the Salmon of Wisdom, and I'm not saying I am, you see. But if I was, I wonder what I would tell you to do?"

He was silent once more. In fact, as the minutes continued to pass without another word from him, the girls began to think that certainly this time he had fallen asleep.

All the while, they and he were drifting along in the water. But now their little boat drew close to a bend in the river, and at the very edge of a mossy bank, they suddenly came upon an old gnarled tree.

Meghan whispered more to herself than anyone else, "How *beautiful* it is."

At first sight Kate saw only its knots and gnarls. She thought it must be the oldest tree imaginable. But with Meghan's words, suddenly she could see the tree quite differently. Yes, it was beautiful beyond description. How had she not seen that before? What was it the salmon had said, "*A loss may provide its own advantage*"? Perhaps, thought Kate, this had something to do with what he had tried to explain to Meghan.

"You can pick the nuts that fall from the tree," said the salmon.

His words quite startled them. He had been quiet for so long, they had almost forgotten him as they both gazed at the beautiful hazelnut tree.

Chapter Three

ALREADY THE little boat was drawing itself so near the bank that all Kate need do was climb out to reach dry land. Meanwhile, Meghan looked to secure the boat. A fallen log had long ago driven its way into the bank, and she fastened the mooring rope around it.

As Kate came up to the tree, the great trunk quivered, its limbs drew themselves away from her, and the leaves rustled, though there was nary a breeze. She looked back at her sister and the salmon, full of uncertainty, not knowing what was expected of her.

"The great, old fellow has forgotten all about people," said the salmon. "Here then, let me speak to him a moment." And turning toward the tree, he rose a little out of the water, saying, "It's all right, my soul. I daresay, she's not about to go picking nuts without your leave. Are you, dear? Tell him so, that's a good girl."

When Kate hesitated, the salmon urged her on. "Now, now, Kate. Don't be shy, dear. He *is* waiting, after all."

"I beg your pardon," said Kate, not knowing quite where on the huge tree to look while addressing him. She finally decided to fix her gaze on the trunk, that is to say, just below where the great heavy boughs begin to rise. "I won't pick even one nut without your permission. I can assure you of that with all my heart, my lord."

At a loss to say anything else, she turned back, looking to the salmon for guidance.

"Very good," the salmon told Kate in his usual slow, calm voice. Presently, he resumed speaking to the ancient tree. "Do what you can for the child, won't you, old thing. These two girls have such a lot to accomplish before their adventure comes to a close. They could use your help, you see."

The tree relaxed its branches, and its delicate leaves curled back to face Kate. Then, while she watched, all at once the great tree shook itself, and suddenly a cascade of nuts fell down onto the mossy ground at her feet.

"There you are, my dear," said the salmon. "You see what a good fellow he is. It's quite all right to pick them now. Quick as you can then and we'll be off. It's getting dark, I'm afraid, and you both had better be on your way."

When she had picked up every last one, Kate made a proper, royal curtsy just as her governess had taught her. After all, she was a princess and

knew she must not forget her manners, regardless of how extraordinary the situation.

"Thank you, my lord," said Kate. "My sister, Meghan, and I are deeply grateful for your generosity."

The tree stretched one long bough down toward Kate and gently brushed her flame-red hair. Suddenly she felt a current of warmth flowing through her from the top of her head to the tips of her fingers and toes. Why, it was as if the tree had hugged her. She spread her arms as wide as they could stretch and then she hugged the tree. She had not made up her mind to do it. No, indeed not. It even surprised her. But doing it made her ever so glad. Then, with a shy smile and admittedly the trace of a blush, she hurried back to her sister and quickly stepped into the boat.

The girls waved and thanked the ancient tree again as the little boat pushed off from the bank. They were drifting once more, and silently the salmon swam along beside them. Now and then, both girls looked back at the tree. At their last sight of him, the sun was setting behind his outspread branches and each leaf shone silver in the waning light.

Then a breeze came up from over the yonder hills. Every leaf shimmered and two broke free. Carried by the breeze, they floated, swaying this way and that as graceful as two dancers. But in a few moments they fell lightly, one leaf following

the other, upon the water. Now the river took them up, and merrily they hurried on their way.

"I'll be leaving you now," said the old salmon.

"But how can you?" exclaimed the sisters. "You haven't told us what we must do."

"Haven't I?" asked the salmon in return. "Well, I don't know that I can. As a rule I don't give advice. *Suggestions*, perhaps. But never advice."

He was starting to slow his pace. Their boat was moving faster and the space separating them grew wider and wider.

"Oh, please," Kate pleaded, beginning to feel desperate. "Won't you suggest a direction for us, if nothing else?"

"One direction is as good as another. It's nearly impossible to avoid one's destiny, you know. But I should think that this little boat will take you some-where or other. It's done quite well so far, wouldn't you say?"

"But, oh, really," said Meghan. "We would be so grateful for just a bit of guidance."

"It is very hard to refuse you, my dear," replied the salmon, farther away from them than ever. "Very well. There is one thing. Keep in mind that one should concern oneself with practical matters. Yes, even when unusual events are taking place. And so, you might do well to seek some means of employment, or else how will you be able to look after yourselves?

"Now, at a certain point your little boat will stop drifting. There's a fine old castle at the end of the path leading away from the river not far from where you should be getting out. You might consider following that path. If you had a mind to, I'm sure one or both of you could find work there. They are good people, though they've seen their own share of troubles recently.

"And now, my dears, I really should say no more. Good-bye, then," said the old salmon. And with that he leapt out of the water seemingly as light and as young as a newborn. There was a flash of bright silver, and he dove back into the water. They didn't see him again.

Chapter Four

T WAS STRANGE to be without the salmon. Truly, both girls suddenly felt quite lonely, but neither wanted to admit just how much they missed him already. Instead, they kept silent for a time. The light was fading, and they knew it would soon be night.

"Why, if he wasn't the most exasperating creature, I'm sure I don't know who is," announced Kate, at last. "Now, what's to be done? I had so hoped he would help us."

"Perhaps he has," said Meghan in a low voice.

In the gathering shadows Kate could scarcely make out her sister's figure, sitting opposite her in the boat. "Oh, dear Meghan, how can you say that? Here we've come all this way and all we have to show for it are these hazelnuts." Kate dug them out of her pocket and counted them. "Nine hazelnuts in all. Well, do you suppose if we ate them we'd grow wise?"

"Maybe," replied Meghan. "But I don't think we should eat them. At least not just yet."

"I suppose you're right," said Kate, putting them

back in her pocket. "I don't know what's to become of us now, though."

Just then Meghan sat straight up in the boat. "Look, Kate! Can you see? We're drifting toward land again."

It was true, and in a few moments the little boat had run aground. The sisters stepped out onto a sandy bank and began to climb up toward level ground. At the very top, a path continued into a dark, brooding grove of tall evergreens, and they followed it. It was damp as they walked, and a mist rose up from the forest floor and hung in midair just above the low hedges.

Soon they came to a fork in the path. The girls stopped, wondering which direction to choose, left or right.

"You decide," Kate told Meghan.

"Well, the salmon told us that one direction was as good as another. So I expect we can take either without making a serious mistake."

"Not true! Not true! Take the wrong path and you'll regret it," came a voice seemingly from nowhere.

"What?" said Kate, with surprise. "Who said that?"

"Who, indeed! Why, me, of course. What a silly question," replied the voice.

The girls peered through the mist into the shrubbery, but searching proved quite futile. "Per-

haps you could tell us which way we *should* go?" asked Meghan.

"Well, that depends on what you're looking for, doesn't it?" said the voice.

"Honestly," said Kate, "I don't mean to be rude, but if you have something to tell us, I do wish you'd come out in the open and say it."

"Why didn't you say that in the first place? I'm right here."

On closer inspection they discovered a salamander, lying on his stomach, beneath the leafy branches of a privet hedge at the crossroads. His rear legs were stretched out behind him, and his two front legs were straight ahead of him, rather like a sphinx would sit, thought both girls.

There was a dreamy look in his eyes, and now and then he slowly lifted his long tail, held it up for a moment or two, and then let it drop upon the soft ground. But it was his costume that seemed most remarkable, for he wore a fireproof topcoat and a matching vest of a shiny silver material. On his head he wore a fire helmet, and coiled neatly at his side were several lengths of sturdy fire hose.

"Has there been a fire?" asked Kate.

"Why, do you expect one?" asked the salamander, beginning to look alarmed.

"Goodness, no," they assured him.

"Well, of course, I knew that," he said. "Never mind, though. I'm prepared should there be one."

"That *is* a relief," said Meghan. Then, wishing to return to the issue of which path to choose, she cleared her throat and said, "Now, then, if you would—"

But Kate couldn't resist interrupting. All this talk of fire had made her curious. "Are there many fires here in the forest?" she asked.

"Certainly not! Gracious me, I should say *not*! Why ever would you ask such a thing? What a girl for questions!" remarked the salamander.

"Then, why on earth are you dressed in such a fashion?"

"My dear girl, it is expected of me, isn't it? I can't think of a time when people didn't expect *salamanders* to concern themselves with fire. They say we're born from the flames or that we live within the fire or that we simply can extinguish it. For pity's sake, they've even been known to throw us into it to prove their point! Frankly, we don't know a thing about it. But we do feel obliged to uphold the myth as best we can. There are so few around these days."

"Salamanders or myths?" asked Kate.

"Both, of course."

"I'm sure you're right there," said Meghan, growing impatient. "But perhaps we could return to the question of which path we should take."

"I'd be happy to," replied the salamander. "If you take the *left* path, and I strongly advise against

it, you'll soon find your way into the domain of Argante, the queen of Faerie. You would regret it, I assure you. She is a merciless monarch, and her subjects are full of wicked mischief. But if you take the *right* path, you're bound to reach the castle where I imagine you were headed in the first place."

"Why, yes," said Kate. "We hope to find work there."

"Well, then, the path to the right is the one you want."

"Thank you so much," said the two girls.

"You're quite welcome, I'm sure," replied the salamander as he rose to his feet. "And now, I'm afraid, I must bid you adieu, for the hour is late and I should be running along."

Chapter Five

HE GIRLS WERE not more than a few steps upon the new path when Kate stopped. "Now, do you suppose he meant *our* right or *his* right?"

"Perhaps we should go back and ask him," suggested Meghan. "He can't have gone very far since we said good-bye."

When they returned, the salamander was nowhere to be found. They called after him, but there was no reply. By now it was quite dark, the moon was not yet visible, and the girls agreed there was nothing else to do but proceed in the same direction as before.

Time passed and they continued, but wherever shadows fell an unknown presence seemed to linger, watching and waiting. Indeed, the night wood was full of small noises, song and chatter, cries and rustling. Constantly each girl started at what seemed a sudden clear call, supposing for an instant that it was meant for her alone.

At last the moon lifted with slow majesty, and everything was bathed in silver. They began to see

36

hollow trees and hedges washed clean of dark mystery, radiant now with moonlight. Relieved, they stopped to rest and soon slept fitfully.

Near dawn, a bird sang out and was still again. The sound woke them, and rubbing their eyes, they got to their feet. A breeze brushed past and set the leaves rustling. Suddenly Kate looked up and listened with a passionate intensity. Meghan took her hand and studied her face with curiosity.

"Did you see him?" Kate whispered.

"Who?" Meghan asked.

"The young man." Kate sighed. "He's gone, now. But, Meghan, he was so beautiful. Like a prince bathed in silver light, strange and haunting. Yet I wasn't afraid."

For a long while, she was silent. But presently she began again. "Oh, now, Meghan! Do you hear it? Such music I never dreamed to hear. Listen, it's like the sweetest bells. Surely it's not far off. Come, we must follow."

Meghan, greatly perplexed, held back, reluctant to obey. "I hear nothing, myself," she said, "but the wind playing in the reeds and leaves."

Kate never answered, if indeed she had heard. Rapt, she was possessed in all her senses by this new feeling which caught her up and drew her helpless soul in a strong sustaining grasp.

Meghan held her hand more firmly, refusing to move or let go. But Kate broke free and ran this

way and that, chasing after the sound. Heedless, she pushed through undergrowth, blossoms, and scented herbage until finally she came to a hill all covered with vines and sweet grasses of a marvelous green. There she stopped, transfixed.

Light was breaking through the trees when Meghan caught up to her, and there were tears in Kate's eyes as she spoke. "Fainter and fainter still. Until now, I have lost it altogether. Oh, Meghan, I shall never see him again, and the music that might have led me to him has vanished."

Breathless, Meghan put one hand on her sister's shoulder, and her stolid presence steadied Kate. At last, Meghan said, "Hush, dear. Perhaps you will. But it is my guess that the figure you saw and the music you heard were Faerie magic. I fear we have taken the wrong path, after all.

"Now come away from here. The sight of this hill makes me uneasy. I feel it's no ordinary spot. No, indeed," concluded Meghan with a shiver of dread.

Somehow she knew this hill to be a threshold to the realm of Faerie, though she would not dare say this aloud. Fearful that they might be drawn in at any moment, she wished to get Kate away. Certainly nightfall was the most dangerous, but even now with the sun shining, she felt the ominous presence of this other world's power all around them.

Kate gave no further resistance, and silently

she turned to follow Meghan. There was no point in giving up the path now, they had come too far to turn back. Consoling themselves that the worst was over, they hurried on. About midmorning their perseverance was rewarded. The forest grew thin, and through the trees they saw in the distance the majestic turrets of a stone castle. Convinced that this was the very castle they were seeking, they quickened their pace.

Chapter Six

EARY AND HUNGRY, they soon arrived at the great wood and iron drawbridge which stretched across a wide moat, encircling the castle. Crossing it, Kate pulled at the heavy chain, summoning the doorkeeper.

When it was learned that the two girls were in need of work and shelter, they were ushered into the kitchen. There they met Old Nell, a little woman in a faded blue gown who presided over all such matters.

In the first few days of their arrival, Old Nell looked after them with loving kindness as she did everyone else in the castle. It was she who arranged for Kate to work with her in the kitchen, and when she found that Meghan was an artist with a needle and thread, she gave her the task of mending the fine royal linens. The two princesses accepted what was offered without complaint, and took up lodging in an attic chamber tucked away in one of the castle towers.

Not long after, on a windy night when work was done and the two girls sat beside the hearth

with Old Nell, they began to tell her the story of their adventure. She listened with great interest, but when she learned that they had passed through the forbidden part of the forest, she was very much horrified and surprised that no harm had come to them.

Looking closely at both of them, she said, "You two must have some powerful charm to protect you."

Their story prompted her to recount the sad events surrounding the castle, for a little less than a year ago, on All Hallows' Eve, the night that in ancient times was known as Samhain Eve, the king's eldest son had vanished without a trace in that same part of the forest.

"Aye, it was a tragic day for all of us," she told them. "On that morning the princes, Miles, the elder, and Gwyn, the younger, rode out into the forest. But when late that night neither returned, the master grew worried and sent out horsemen with torches to search for them. At dawn Gwyn was found, but his brother was never to return."

Old Nell shook her head and blinked back the tears in her eyes. "I rocked both boys in their cradle when they were babes. Their good mother was frail, and not long after the youngest was born she passed away. And so as they grew it was to me they came to tell their troubles and to share their joy. They are like my own sons, they are. No mother could love them more or know them better."

"But, dear Nell," pleaded Kate, "does anyone know for certain what happened that day?"

"I tell you *I* know, though the master might refuse to believe it," answered Nell as she wiped her nose with the end of her apron. "The young prince was sick with fever when they brought him to me. I nursed Gwyn through that night, and his talk was wild. But what I learned was this, that he and Miles had come upon a white deer while riding in the forest that morning. They chased it throughout the day, but they came no closer than at first. Then, at twilight, Gwyn lost sight of both the deer and his older brother, who was by far the better rider of the two.

"Aye, but that was no ordinary deer, to be sure! Those from the world beyond our own sent it to lure the two princes."

"The world beyond our own," repeated Meghan in a hushed tone. "Yes, I think I understand. But who are they? Do they have a name?"

"They go by many names, child. My granny called them the *sidhe*. Then, some call them the Faerie folk, but that doesn't suit them none, for it's too sweet a name for such creatures. It's the *sidhe* that took Prince Miles. Their queen is fond of capturing young knights to add to her court.

"Mind though, when the fever finally broke, young Gwyn could tell me nothing more. But he blamed himself, thinking that if he hadn't lost sight of his brother, all would have been different.

"Desperate to make things right, he returned time and again to the forest. But it was all for nothing, for there was nary a clue to follow. Then strange stories sprang up, people came back from the wood, declaring they had seen Prince Miles. Peasant girls, in particular, swore they had met him in the wood and spoken to him. Indeed, the tales soon enough grew frightful as they can when a thing cannot be put to rest. Finally, hoping to bring it all to a close, the master forbade anyone, most especially his own son, to venture into that part of the forest.

"And so, my lord will hear nothing more on the matter, not from his son or from me. Only I believe what some of the peasants say to be true. There is a veil between our world and the *sidhe*'s. Here and there, you can find tears where one can pass through. And on All Hallows' Eve, or what the old ones call the Eve of Samhain, these spirits are most powerful."

A gust of wind blew down the chimney and lifted Meghan's scarf for an instant. She shivered, remembering the silence of the hill where she and Kate had stood alone deep in the forest.

"Kate saw a young man, a prince she called him. Didn't you, dear?"

For some time now Kate had been staring at the flames in the hearth, lost in her own thoughts. Without looking up, she nodded yes.

44

"It was nearly dawn when she saw him," continued Meghan. "I thought then that he belonged to what you call the *sidhe*."

Later that evening when the two girls were alone in their bedchamber, Kate was unusually silent, and Meghan knew that the talk that night had troubled her. When she tried to draw her out, Kate put her arms around her and gave Meghan a quick hug, saying, "You've spent too much time listening to such tales. Come, now. It's late and we should both get some sleep."

But even as the dawning light streamed through the tower windows, Meghan shivered still, remembering the chill of the wind and her premonition about the hill, silent and overgrown as any mound of *sidhe*.

Chapter Seven

HE NEXT EVENING when work was done, Kate slipped away into the woods without a word to Meghan. Old Nell's story had affected her deeply. While she listened, she had become convinced that the missing Prince Miles and the young man she had seen in the forest were one and the same. Even if it meant defying the king's orders, she was determined to go back into the forbidden forest to try to find him.

There was still light enough to see, but the moon was not yet up as she retraced her steps. She was looking for the hill, but time passed and she saw no familiar signs to guide her. She felt she was going in circles, and when she returned to the same spot time and time again, she grew discouraged. Deciding to rest before starting out once more, she sat down and leaned against the trunk of a hollowed-out tree.

While she had been searching, the forest seemed unusually silent, as though it were waiting for something to happen. Now, she, too, began to listen intently. So that when she heard the sudden snap of a branch, she jumped with a start. The sound

must have come from nearby, but she was too startled to be sure. Then there was another snap, and suddenly the prince stood before her.

"Have you been waiting for me?" he asked.

Kate hardly had breath to answer, but finally she stammered, "Yes."

"I know you," he said, looking more closely at her.

As he did Kate was struck by his blue-gray eyes, for they seemed lit with a cool, unnerving glow. She was not able to pull her gaze away.

"You were in the forest not long ago," he continued. "I saw you with another girl. It was nearly dawn."

"I've come back for you," Kate blurted out, and she stretched out her hand to take his.

He didn't pull away, but neither did he take her hand. Instead, he asked, "What is it you have in your pocket?"

Kate was surprised by the question. Unconsciously she had been holding the hazelnuts which were still in the pocket of her gown.

"They're nuts," she replied. "Hazelnuts. Why do you ask?"

But the prince didn't answer. He shook his head, and turning, he looked away into the darkness.

Was he looking for someone? Kate wondered. Did he think someone was watching them?

In a moment he turned back to her. "There is

nothing more I'd rather do than return with you. And perhaps you are the one who can save me."

"Yes!" exclaimed Kate. "I know it's true. Please, let us go at once."

He shook his head. "I can't," he said. "It's not that simple. There must be a sacrifice. One would have to be very brave to save me."

"Brave?" repeated Kate. "What do you mean?"

"It would take someone who loved me enough to risk her *own* life."

"I do," said Kate, at once blushing at her own boldness.

"There would be a test," continued the prince.

"Tell me what must be done and I'll do it," answered Kate, standing up and smoothing the creases from her gown. "I've been through a good deal already. I daresay I could meet the challenge. But you must tell me what it is."

"All right," the prince said with the first trace of a smile to cross his lips since they had met. But as he resumed speaking his expression grew solemn again. "If you truly mean to save me, then tomorrow on the Eve of Samhain, you must come to the grove of the nine dead trees. You see, Lady Kate, I have no time to lose, for I shall never have another chance.

"In the dark when twelve strikes mark the dead hour of midnight, those that hold me will take their horses into the grove for a great feast. If you

love me as you say, if lady you are to win me, then you must risk all and come alone."

"I will, I swear it. But how will I know you in the darkness among all the rest?"

"When the first troop comes riding by, do nothing, let them pass. When the next troop comes do the same. Then the third troop will come; I'll be one of those. Let the black horse pass, my lady, and ignore the brown. But quickly grasp the silver-gray steed and pull his rider down.

"For I'll be riding the silver horse, and my right hand will be gloved and my left will be bare. My cape will be gray, my lady. These signs I'll give you.

"But take heed of what I say, my lady. Listen, for I'll warn you now. They'll turn me while you hold me into things you never dreamed. But hold me nonetheless or we shall both be doomed. Hold me fast till day is dawning, if it is as you say and I am your own true love."

"I shall never have another," whispered Kate.

"Nor I, Lady Kate. But if you change your mind or if you fail me, I'll understand."

Before Kate could answer, he stepped back into the shadows and suddenly he was gone. It was as though he had never been there.

The moon was high as she made her way back to the castle. It was very late when last she reached her own bed at the top of the tower. She was relieved that everyone, even Meghan, was still asleep.

Indeed, she didn't know what she would have said had she been discovered. There was an hour or so before daybreak. She should sleep, she told herself, but her mind was so full of wild thoughts that it didn't seem possible. Yet before her head touched the pillow she was fast asleep.

Chapter Eight

LOOMY WAS THE night and eerie the gloss upon the grass as Kate donned her green cloak and walked into the wood the next evening. It was the Eve of Samhain when the veil between the realm of Faerie and the realm of man is drawn apart and anything can happen.

About the hour of midnight she stepped into the grove of the nine dead trees, nearby stood the Faerie mound, silent and still. The moonlight came silver through the mist, as if she had passed beyond the veil of her own world into an enchanted realm. The air lay motionless. She felt its pressure against her skin and knew that something outside her understanding was with her in the grove. She listened for a sound but heard nothing. And then in the next instant, there was the ring of a bridle. Though her heart began to race, she was as glad of it as any earthly sound she had ever heard.

Clutching at the hazelnuts hidden in her pocket, she stared as suddenly a thousand points of light appeared and began to grow larger and larger. Danc-

ing above the mass of shadows, they came thunder-
ing out of the Faerie mound. And so came the hosts
of Faerie, moving through the air on the Eve of
Samhain. Would they see her? She felt the hair rise
on her arms at the sight of them.

There before her was the white glimmer of a
horse and a flash of gold from a rider's reins trailed
by still other riders with torches blazing in their
hands. Around a curve and up the slope of the hill
they swept past without a glance at her, sparkling
with a fierce, unearthly beauty.

As they entered the grove, Kate thought, Is he
there among them? Oh, please, by all the heavens,
let it be so tonight!

Then she saw Argante, the queen of Faerie,
mounted on a raven-black steed. In the torchlight
her hair shone like rippling black water, and her
eyes glittered hard and bright as diamonds. Kate
knew at once with chilling certainty that if she
failed tonight there would be no mercy from this
cruel queen.

But there was no time for fear. The riders were
all around her. Hoofbeats thundered in her ears,
and the torches showered sparks like falling stars.
Her heart was pounding. She let the black horse
pass, then ignored the brown, but then the queen's
horse pulled to a halt, and other riders sprang off
their mounts to stand at her side.

Just then Kate saw him—the silver knight bal-

anced on his rearing silver-gray horse. He raised his streaming torch high, and she saw that his right hand was gloved and his left was bare. His silver cloak was thrown back. The moving light flared from the silver threads in his thin tunic, and on his arm-rings and neck-torque, and from the silver circlet that held his shining hair.

There was no turning back for her. She grasped the silver-gray steed's bridle and pulled the rider down. As the bridle fell there was a ghastly cry, and the others shouted in one voice, *"He is stolen from us!"*

Never daring to loosen her hold upon the prince, Kate looked down into his eyes and saw instead a scaly serpent coiling in her grip. But she held him fast and didn't let him go, telling herself all the while, I will not fail you now or ever, for you are my own true love.

In a flash of lightning the serpent disappeared, and in its place Kate held a vicious bear and then a hungry lion. But still she held him to her and would not let him go.

And just as quickly he was turned into a red-hot iron, but though he burned her flesh and bones, she held him tight and would not falter.

And next she held a giant toad, then suddenly a fire-breathing dragon. But hold him still she did and would not let him go even if it meant her death.

The dragon vanished, and a screaming eagle took its place, then a swan with wild, spread wings, and last Kate held a young sleeping man, reborn into the mortal world—the transformation was complete. She covered him with her long green cloak as tenderly as if he were a babe, and touched his lips with hers. His eyes opened and he was himself again.

Just then the queen spoke out, "She has taken away the fairest in my company, a noble knight. Had I but known how the matter would be won, I'd have struck out his eyes of gray and put in two of wood. Indeed, had I but known before he came into this grove tonight, I'd have ripped out his heart of flesh and put in one of stone."

Kate took a breath and said, "I have won him fair, Majesty. And now it is my right to ask a boon."

" 'Tis true enough, lady," answered the queen, but her lips were tight and her glance was cold. "Ask what you will, though you will gain no greater prize than the one you've already won."

"Give me a means to restore my sister, so she can be herself once more."

The queen fixed Kate with an icy smile before answering, "This boon I cannot grant. To do what you ask, you must have a branch from a living hazelnut tree." The queen threw back her black satin cloak and stretched out her arms, pointing toward the

dead trees that stood like stones in a circle around them. "As you can see, lady, they are all quite dead. Meghan must remain as your mother has made her."

"Kate has the means to bring the grove back to life, Your Highness," said Miles, and turning toward Kate, he asked, "You do have the hazelnuts, don't you? Well, then, dear Kate, take them out so she can see them for herself."

Kate reached down into her pocket and drew out her small treasure of nuts. The entire Faerie company gasped in wonder as she opened her hand; there were nine hazelnuts just as there were nine dead hazelnut trees standing in the grove.

"Give them here," the queen demanded.

"Wait!" cautioned Miles. "Will you help her, Your Majesty?"

"If she can make my grove live again, I will grant her a branch from one of these trees," replied the queen.

What does it all mean? wondered Kate. How is it possible that I can make this grove come alive in one night?

As though Miles could read her thoughts, he squeezed her hand, and leaning close he whispered, "Don't doubt the magic of this night, Kate. To-night, you have the power to restore the grove. Go now and place one hazelnut deep into the roots of each dead tree."

She took strength from his words, and breaking away from the host of riders, Kate began to dig down into the dry and dusty roots of the first dead tree. She worked hurriedly, placing one after the other into the earth, until the nine nuts were planted. Only then did she step back to see what she had done.

A hush had fallen over the company. All eyes were fixed on the circle of trees. The pulse of life was already flowing through the grove. Kate could almost feel it. The branches of each tree trembled as they began to sprout young green buds. In the cool moonlight, suddenly new leaves emerged from the tender buds. The sacred grove in all its splendor was restored.

"A miracle!" exclaimed Kate, quite unable to believe her eyes.

"On the Eve of Samhain, all things are possible," said the queen. "Now, then. Take what is your due and go in peace before I change my mind."

Kate broke a branch from the nearest hazelnut tree. Then hand in hand she and Miles turned from the Faerie company and walked out of the grove.

When they reached the castle Kate had one thought only. She must get up to the attic chamber to Meghan. Together, she and Miles climbed the stone steps to the very top of the tower. There they found Meghan, still asleep.

Gently Kate touched Meghan's sheep's head

with the hazelnut rod, once, twice, and then a third time. Meghan stirred and began to wake. Turning her head toward Kate, the linen scarf came away, revealing Meghan's own beautiful, young face.

Kate began to weep tears of joy and relief at the blessed sight of her sister. "Oh, Meghan! We are saved. My dear beloved sister, the spell is broken! Come, see for yourself." She pulled Meghan from the bed, and the two princesses stood before the looking glass.

Hardly able to believe what she saw in the mirror, Meghan gasped and put her hands to her face. She was indeed herself again, and throwing her arms around Kate, she, too, began to weep with joy.

Chapter Nine

OW THE KING and his brother welcomed the eldest son! They welcomed him with kisses and questions. They welcomed him with feasting and dancing and song. They believed him dead and there he was, their own, standing before them. But Old Nell knew better, and when there was a moment she pulled Kate to her side and squeezed her and kissed her and looked deep into her eyes.

"All that could save him from enchantment was the unyielding grasp of a mortal lover, given at midnight on All Hallows' Eve. And you did it, my noble-hearted Kate. You risked your own mortal soul to win him. Glory be, girl! You are the bravest of us all."

The year of dread and sorrow was at an end. Kate and Miles were wed, and a great feast was held for them, full of laughter and music. And in the weeks that followed, is it any wonder that Meghan and Prince Gwyn fell deeply in love?

Then one night, not long after Meghan was wed to Gwyn, curiously both sisters had the identi-

cal dream. Together, they were standing on the mossy bank of the river. Before them was the ancient hazelnut tree in all its splendor, and directly behind them in the cool, dark river swam the salmon.

"We've come back," Meghan was saying.

"I knew you would," the salmon answered in his slow, gentle voice they had come to love.

"You see, I'm a real girl again. Thanks to Kate and *you*. But Kate had to sacrifice the hazelnuts to break the spell. She did it for me, although she knew it meant giving up our one gift of wisdom."

While Meghan was speaking it had grown quite dark, and all the light there was flowed from the salmon. Kate thought, He looks like a giant star in the river of night.

"There, there, my soul," said the salmon. "Don't fret. You must listen now and remember, *love provides its own wisdom*."

All the rest of their days, Kate and Meghan were never to forget his words.